FIRST LIGHT

For my son, Joel, who has taught me so much.
Gary Crew

For Mum and Dad, who took me fishing and let me fly.
Peter Gouldthorpe

For a free color catalog describing Gareth Stevens Publishing's list of high-quality books
and multimedia programs, call 1-800-542-2595 (USA) or 1-800-461-9120 (Canada).
Gareth Stevens Publishing's Fax: (414) 225-0377.
See our catalog, too, on the World Wide Web: http://gsinc.com

Library of Congress Cataloging-in-Publication Data

Crew, Gary, 1947-
First light / written by Gary Crew ; illustrated by Peter Gouldthorpe.
p. cm. -- "First published in 1993 by Lothian Publishing Co."
Summary: A young boy, who would rather spend time with his model airplanes, reluctantly
accompanies his father on a fishing trip that starts before the first light of day.
ISBN 0-8368-1664-1 (lib. bdg.)
[1. Fishing--Fiction. 2. Boats and boating--Fiction. 3. Fathers
and sons--Fiction.] I. Gouldthorpe, Peter, ill. II. Title.
PZ7.C867Fi   1996
[E]--dc20   96-31213

First published in North America in 1996 by
Gareth Stevens Publishing
1555 North RiverCenter Drive, Suite 201
Milwaukee, Wisconsin 53212 USA

First published in 1993 by Lothian Publishing Co. Pty. Ltd., 11 Munro Street, Port Melbourne,
Victoria 3207, Australia. Text © 1993 by Gary Crew. Illustrations © 1993 by Peter Gouldthorpe.

Printed in the United States of America

1 2 3 4 5 6 7 8 9 01 00 99 98 97 96

FIRST LIGHT

GARY CREW ❖ PETER GOULDTHORPE

Gareth Stevens Publishing
MILWAUKEE

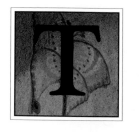he boy worked in his room, alone and happy. Spread around him were the plans of the aircraft he was building. This was no plastic model made from a toy shop kit, but a prototype, designed by the boy himself. The single wing made of pale gray silk stretched over balsa wood was three feet from tip to tip. It was so light, the boy could balance it on his fingertips.

The boy smiled. If he worked late, at least until midnight, he would be finished. In the morning, at first light when the air was still, he would take the plane to the park to test it. Only then could he be sure it would fly.

He set the wing down. "Good," he said to himself, "perfect." But as he leaned forward, ready to continue, he sensed someone behind him.

"Are you done?" his father asked.

"Nearly," the boy nodded.

His father came closer, blocking the light. "Aren't you forgetting something?"

"What?" the boy asked.

"Tomorrow," his father answered. "I'm taking you fishing, remember? And there's the tackle to be fixed." He went to the door and stopped. "Now."

In the morning, the boy was awakened by the screaming kettle. His room was dark. He lifted his arm to peer at the luminous face of his wristwatch. Four a.m. He sighed and turned to the wall, half-listening to the muffled voices of his parents in the kitchen. First his father, complaining, then his mother: "Leave him alone. He wants to finish that plane . . ."

His father cut her off. "That plane? That plane? Always the same old story. It's not normal, stuck in there. He needs to get out, like other kids . . . When I was his age . . . ."

angrove branches sprang back and struck the boy across the face, stinging his cheeks, making his eyes smart. Khaki-colored mud filled his shoes, but he kept on. He gripped his fishing rod in one hand, a net in the other. Lumbering through the trees ahead of him his father whistled, joking about the cold and the mud. The boy heard but did not respond. He looked at his father's back and let his anger grow; his father so big in his duffle coat, a black mass blocking the boy's view as they headed for the dinghy, out there on the open water.

"This is the life," the father said. "This is what you need. Adventure."

But the boy hated it. He hated having to follow, as boys do — to be taught the things their fathers like. He longed for his room at home — for his designs and models; for the smooth, bright surface of silver instruments; for the sharp, spiced scent of freshly trimmed wood.

He sank to his knees in the mud, dropping the net as he grabbed for a branch to save himself. Leathery leaves came away in his hand, and he fell forward, calling "Wait."

His father laughed. "It's only mud," he said. "It washes off."

The boy reached for the net and went on, until the mangroves thinned and he saw the sea.

A wooden dinghy rocked gently on the swell, its anchor rope sagging beneath bunches of dripping weeds.

"Get that anchor," his father said, and the boy waded out, intending to obey. But as he leaned forward to place the rod and tackle in the prow, the dinghy lurched and turned.

The boy cried out as the anchor rope stretched taut, ripping at the skin of his leg. The tackle fell from his grasp, clattering into the hull of the boat.

At the stern where he was waiting, the father shook his head and turned away.

When they had cast off, the boy took his place in the prow and listened for the rhythmic dip and spread of the oars behind him. He sighed and rested his arms on the gunwale. *The surface of the sea is a skin*, he thought, *a smooth, silky skin.* He was tempted to reach out and touch it but was afraid. *It's different from the skin of my plane. This moves like a creature, like a creature breathing.*

A sudden shiver passed over him, and he pulled back.

The oars spread and dipped for the last time, then folded.

"This is it," his father called. "Where the big ones live. Let the anchor go. And be quiet."

The boy reached down to grip the cold iron shaft of the anchor and lifted it over the side. He lowered it slowly, hand over hand, feeling the coarse, wet rope rasp against the tender skin of his palms, until it hung limp. *The anchor is on the bottom,* he thought, and tied the rope off.

The dinghy shuddered, turned, ran with the current, and was still.

"What's the time?"

The boy looked at his watch. "Five-fifteen."

His father grunted. "That gives us an hour until the sun hits the water. Pass down that creel."

The boy did as he was told, then leaned back against the gunwale, watching. His father bit through the fishing line, threaded two lead sinkers, then attached a trace of heavier gut. He sorted through the tackle box and chose a hook, checking that the shank was straight, the barb sharp. Finally, he drew a knife from the sheath on his belt and sliced the tentacles of a squid, skewering a lump of mottled flesh with the hook. "OK," he said, and swung the rod back to cast.

The line snaked out over the slow swell, pierced the surface, and sank. "Well," the father said. "What's the matter with you?"

The boy shrugged. "I'll wait for a minute," he said. "I'll see how you do first."

His father shook his head. "You'd better not wait too long. When that sun hits the water, that's it. No good fishing with the sun on the water."

They sat in silence. From time to time, the father reeled in to freshen his bait, then cast out again.

The boy stared at the sea. *I could take the knife and cut it*, he thought, *like silk, like skin* . . . and he would have, but his father stiffened and sat up, lifting the fishing rod high.

"What?" the boy said.

"I've got one," his father laughed. The rod arched almost double, its tip dipping toward the water. "Get the net. Get the net!"

The net was in the bottom of the boat where the boy had dropped it. He grabbed its handle, but it would not move. It was stuck beneath an oar.

"Quick," his father yelled. "Now!"

The boy crouched, struggling to lift the oar, aware of the urgency, afraid that he would fail. "It's stuck," he said. "The net's stuck under . . ."

"Watch out!" the father cried. The line ran wild, humming, stretching — until it broke. "Watch out . . ."

is words were lost as the dinghy lifted. It rose from the sea, groaning and shuddering. For a moment it rocked, balancing, then slid back silently, and was still.

The father gripped the seat. The boy knelt, his hands clenched around his father's wrist. There on the surface, the bloodied head of a fish appeared, one pearly eye staring sightless at the sky.

The boy shrank back.

"I hooked it," his father whispered. "I was reeling it in ready for the net, then . . ."

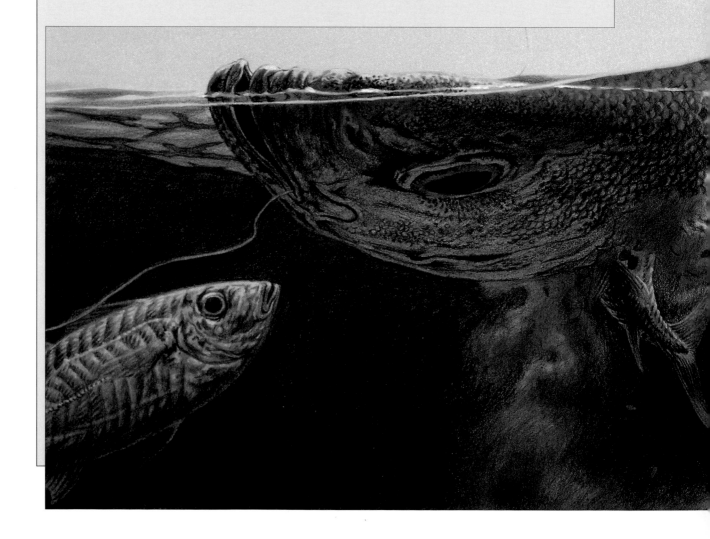

"Then what?" the boy asked.

"Something came up and took it. Something big. So big it lifted the boat," the father replied.

The boy felt water swirling around his feet. "We're leaking," he said.

"It's seepage," the father muttered. "A seam must have opened when we lifted." He pushed the rod away and turned to free the oars. "Get the anchor. We'll go."

At once, the boy scrambled forward to grasp the rope.

But as he reached out toward the surface, he hesitated, thinking *Something big is down there. Something big and black and awful.*

His father was waiting, his broad back hunched over the spread oars.

The boy tried again. But when he looked, he was more certain. There *was* something.

"I can't," he said.

His father released the oars and looked back. He saw his son's fear. "I'll do it," he said, understanding.

He moved to the prow, and the boy made room. The boy took his
father's seat, working the oars to steady the dinghy as the rope came in.
It coiled in the water at their feet.

The boy stood to return to his place, but his father shook his head,

stopping him. "Davey," he said, sitting beside him. "See, it's almost dawn. We'd get back faster if we each took an oar. There's your plane, remember?"

The boy looked toward the east.

Together, the oars lifted. Together, they dipped to break the surface of the sea. And as the boat turned, a gull swooped low, the sweeping span of its pale gray wing catching the first clear light of morning.